KIDS HAVE FEELINGS, TOO

Someone Special Died

By Joan Singleton Prestine
Illustrations by Virginia Kylberg

McGraw-Hill
Children's Publishing

McGraw-Hill
Children's Publishing

A Division of The **McGraw·Hill** *Companies*

©2003 McGraw-Hill Children's Publishing

Send all inquiries to:
McGraw-Hill Children's Publishing
8787 Orion Place
Columbus, OH 43240-4027

ISBN 1-57768-682-9

Library of Congress Cataloging-in-Publication Data is on file with the publisher.

Printed in the United States of America.

1 2 3 4 5 6 7 8 9 PHXBK 01 02 03 04 05 06 07 08 09

Someone I love very much just died. I wonder what it will be like without him.

3

We used to go for walks,
and swing,
and skip stones on the pond.
But now he isn't here.

4

We used to play catch,
put together puzzles,
and read books.
But now he isn't here.

I miss him.
I can't believe
I won't ever see
him again.
Sometimes I pretend
he's still alive.

If I had been there, I wouldn't have let him die. But Mom says I couldn't have done anything to help keep him alive.

Mom says
everything dies.
Flowers die. Dogs die.
People die.

11

"What happened when he died?"

14

"His body stopped working."

"**W**here did his body go?"

"**H**is body is buried in the cemetery."

He shouldn't have left me.
I loved him. It's not fair.
Sometimes I feel so mad,
I want to yell,
or hit my pillow,
or slam the door.

Sometimes I feel so sad,
that nothing makes me happy.
I just want to cry and cry.

Sometimes I don't
want to play with anyone.
Not DeAnna. Not Chris.
Not even my dog Corky.
I just want to be alone.

But when I think about
the fun we had together,
I feel better. I want to make a
scrapbook, so I'll always
remember our good times.
In my scrapbook, I'll draw
a picture of us playing catch.
And going for a walk together.
I'll cut out a picture of
a swing from a magazine.
I'll draw me swinging and him
pushing. I'll glue in a piece
from our favorite puzzle.
And I'll write the names of the
books we read together.

He died and I know he won't be coming back. But with my scrapbook, I'll never forget him.

BAMBIE
PETER RABBIT
MERMAID

Discussing *Someone Special Died* with Children

After reading the story, encourage discussion. Children learn from sharing their thoughts and feelings.

Discussion Questions for *Someone Special Died*

- What feelings did the little girl in the story have after the person she loved died?
- What did she remember doing with the person that she loved?
- How did she show she was sad?
- How did she show she was angry? Why do you think she was angry?
- Could she have saved the person she loved from dying? Why not?
- What did she do to help remember her happy feelings about the person that she loved?

Significance of *Someone Special Died* for Children

Sometimes a book will trigger strong feelings in young children, especially if they have experienced a similar situation. If they feel comfortable, encourage children to share their experiences.